Readers

I'm Going To READ!

These levels are used only as guides;
you and your child can best choose a book that's right.

Level 1: Kindergarten–Grade 1 . . . Ages 4–6
- word bank to highlight new words
- consistent placement of text to promote readability
- easy words and phrases
- simple sentences build to make simple stories
- art and design help new readers decode text

Level 2: Grade 1 . . . Ages 6–7
- word bank to highlight new words
- rhyming texts introduced
- more difficult words, but vocabulary is still limited
- longer sentences and longer stories
- designed for easy readability

Level 3: Grade 2 . . . Ages 7–8
- richer vocabulary of up to 200 different words
- varied sentence structure
- high-interest stories with longer plots
- designed to promote independent reading

Level 4: Grades 3 and up . . . Ages 8 and up
- richer vocabulary of more than 300 different words
- short chapters, multiple stories, or poems
- more complex plots for the newly independent reader
- emphasis on reading for meaning

11/07

LEVEL 4

2 4 6 8 10 9 7 5 3 1

Published by Sterling Publishing Co., Inc.
387 Park Avenue South, New York, NY 10016
Text © 2007 by Harriet Ziefert
Illustrations © 2007 by Barry Gott
Distributed in Canada by Sterling Publishing
c/o Canadian Manda Group, 165 Dufferin Street,
Toronto, Ontario, Canada M6K 3H6
Distributed in the United Kingdom by GMC Distribution Services,
Castle Place, 166 High Street, Lewes, East Sussex, England BN7 1XU
Distributed in Australia by Capricorn Link (Australia) Pty. Ltd.
P.O. Box 704, Windsor, NSW 2756, Australia

I'm Going To Read is a trademark of Sterling Publishing Co., Inc.

Library of Congress Cataloging-in-Publication Data

Ziefert, Harriet.
  Class worms / [by Harriet Ziefert] ; pictures by Barry Gott.
    p. cm.—(I'm going to read)
  Summary: On Tuesday, Mr. Bunsen brings in two hundred live animals in a
Styrofoam cooler for class.
  ISBN-13: 978-1-4027-4300-9
  ISBN-10: 1-4027-4300-9
  [1. Worms—Fiction. 2. Schools—Fiction.] I. Gott, Barry, ill. II. Title.

PZ7.Z487Clw 2007
[E]—dc22

                                                                20070015841

Printed in China

Sterling ISBN-13: 978-1-4027-4300-9
ISBN-10: 1-4027-4300-9

For information about custom editions, special sales, premium and
corporate purchases, please contact Sterling Special Sales
Department at 800-805-5489 or specialsales@sterlingpub.com.

Class Worms

Pictures by Barry Gott

STERLING

Sally

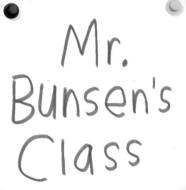

Mr. Bunsen's Class

Matt

Richard

Kelly

Emily

Mr. Bunsen

Jennifer

Jamie

Adam

Justin

Sarah

Chapter One

Red Wigglers

"Good morning, class! It's Tuesday,"
said Mr. Bunsen.

"Good morning, Mr. Bunsen."

"Are you ready to hear the plans for today?"
Mr. Bunsen asked.

"Are we having a picnic?" Sarah asked, eyeing the white Styrofoam cooler in front of Mr. Bunsen.

"No, Sarah. No picnic today! There's not a single peanut-butter-and-jelly sandwich in here—not even one."

"Awwww," groaned everyone.

"Then what is in there?" Sally asked.

"Two hundred live animals!" said Mr. Bunsen.

"Oooh! Can I see?" Kelly begged.

"Those animals must be pretty small!"
shouted Justin.

"They *are* small," Mr. Bunsen said.
"And they don't have fur, or ears,
or even legs."

Sarah, who thought she knew everything,
said, "I know what you have. You have a
bunch of worms!"

"Sarah, this time you are absolutely right!"
said Mr. Bunsen.

Mr. Bunsen lifted the cover of the cooler.
He shoved his hand inside.
He picked up a handful of peat moss and said,
"This is called *worm dirt*."
He walked around the classroom so everybody
could have a good look at the dirt.

"It's moving!" said Sarah.

"Right!" Mr. Bunsen answered. "It's moving because it's alive with red wigglers."

"Yuck!" said Jennifer.

"I bet I know why they're called red wigglers," said Sally. "They're red and they wiggle!"

"Correct," said Mr. Bunsen.

Mr. Bunsen said, "I'll give each of you
a scoopful of dirt on a paper plate."

"Do we *have* to touch the worms?"
Jennifer asked.

"You do," said Mr. Bunsen.
"Worms are harmless. They don't bite.
They don't sting. And they don't talk back."

"You mean like we do!" said Richard.

"Right!" said Mr. Bunsen. "But anyone who
doesn't want to touch worms can handle them
with a plastic spoon. Now, who wants to help
me hand out the worms?"

"I do!" said Jamie.

"I do, too," said Adam.

"Clear your tables, everyone," said Mr. Bunsen.
"Jamie and Adam will give each of you
a plateful of worms."

"This worm likes to crawl under the plate," said Jamie. "It doesn't like it out in the open."

"Why do you think that is?" Mr. Bunsen asked.

"Maybe it's scared," answered Jamie.

"Maybe it's your bad breath!" said Richard. Jamie stuck his tongue out at him.

"What are some other possible reasons?" asked Mr. Bunsen.

"It could be cold," said Kelly.

"Or, it might not like the light," said Sarah.

"Good," said Mr. Bunsen. "Keep thinking and watching and you might find out which answer is correct."

Adam got a magnifying glass.
He watched the worm move for a long time.
He was trying to figure out if the front of the
worm squished together first when it moved,
or if the back did.

Jamie wanted the magnifying glass.
"Give it to me," he said.

"But I'm using it," Adam answered.
"I hardly ever get to use stuff,
and whenever I do, you want it."

"Uh-uh!" Jamie said. "You're the one
who always copies what I do!"

"What's going on?" Mr. Bunsen asked.

"Adam won't share the magnifying glass," Jamie answered.

"I think I know where to find another one," Mr. Bunsen said. "In the meantime, please share."

When Mr. Bunsen walked by, Matt asked,
"Can I measure a worm?"

"What do you think?" Mr. Bunsen asked.

"I think I can," said Matt.
"I think I can do it with a ruler."

"But the worm scrunches up and
   stretches out!" Emily cried.

"Will you measure the worm when it's long
   or when it's short?" Mr. Bunsen asked.

"I guess I'll measure it both ways," said Matt.

"Good idea!" said Mr. Bunsen. "Maybe you can
   find out just how much a worm can stretch."

"That sounds hard!" Matt answered.

"Come on, give it a try," said Mr. Bunsen.

"Can I help?" asked Richard.

"Sure!" said Matt.
   Richard was good at math.
   Matt was happy to have his help.

"Attention everybody! I'm putting some
questions on the board."

Mr. Bunsen found some chalk and wrote:

What happens . . .

when one worm meets another worm?

when a worm bumps into a pencil?

when a worm comes to the edge of a desk?

What happens?

Chapter Two

Worm Experiments

Mr. Bunsen put all kinds of things
on the science table.
There were plastic boxes and jars.
There was plastic tubing, black paper,
tinfoil, tape, and paper cups.
Justin counted four pails, three shovels,
two ant farms—without ants—
and one big washtub.
All of it good stuff for experiments.

"Do worms like hot or do they like cold?" asked Emily.

"I don't know if they like hot or cold," said Matt. "But I know they like puddles."

"How do you know?"

"When it rains, the worms come out and crawl into puddles," answered Matt.

"They all die in the puddles," said Emily.

"They do not. Sometimes there are fifty worms in a puddle, and they're gone the next day," insisted Matt.

Mr. Bunsen heard the conversation.
"Maybe you can make a puddle in this
washtub," said Mr. Bunsen. "Then you can
watch and see if the worms head for
the puddle, or stay in the dirt."

"I think there's something in the water
that worms like," said Matt.

"I think worms are dumb. They head for
puddles, then they drown," said Emily.

"I think you need to find out who's right,"
Mr. Bunsen said.

Adam said he would help Emily and Jamie find out if the worms liked wet or dry soil.

Jamie put wet dirt and dry dirt on different sides of a box. He dumped a handful of worms on the dry side and announced, "I think the worms are going to crawl over to the wet side."

"How do you know?" asked Adam.

"I think Matt's right. Worms like water," answered Jamie.

"I don't think you can be sure until you experiment," said Adam.
Adam felt smart—smarter than Jamie.

Emily said, "I'm going to use sand.
I'll sprinkle half with water and put
my worms on the wet side."

Adam looked at Jamie and Emily and said,
"Since you're starting your worms on
either the dry or the wet side, I'll start mine
in the middle."

"Good idea," said Mr. Bunsen.
"But I have two questions."

"What are they?" Adam asked Mr. Bunsen.

*"Is your dry soil as dry as Jamie's?
Is your wet soil as wet as Emily's?"*

The questions made Adam stop and think.
And he realized maybe he wasn't as smart
as he thought he was—at least about worms.

"Attention, again," called Mr. Bunsen.
"I'm still hearing questions,
   so I'll add them to the list."
   Do worms live under rocks?
   Do worms eat dirt?
   Do worms chew?
   Do worms make tunnels?
"Now we'll go hunting for answers,"
   said Mr. Bunsen.

"Hunting?"

"Yes, we're going on a worm hunt.
   I'll bring pails and shovels. Line up."

Chapter Three

Going on a Worm Hunt

Mr. Bunsen took the lead.
The class followed him to the vacant lot
next to the school.
Mr. Bunsen looked at his watch and said,
"I'll give you five minutes to find worms.
Just to make it a little more fun,
no tools allowed."
Everybody ran in different directions.

Soon Mr. Bunsen said, "Your five minutes
are up. Come back."

"I found my worm under a rock," said Sarah.

"Mine was under some leaves," said Justin.

"I looked under leaves," said Emily,
"but I didn't find a worm. I found a slug!"

"Yuck!" said Jennifer. "They're so slimy!"

"My worm is long and skinny," said Richard. "I found it when I dug up some dirt."

"No fair!" Matt said.

"Sure it's fair," Mr. Bunsen said. "I said no tools, but I didn't say you couldn't dig with your hands."

"We dug together," said Emily and Jamie.
"And here's our worm!"

"Wow!" said Sally. "That's the biggest worm
  I've ever seen. It must be six inches!"

"Don't be silly!" said Sarah. "It's big,
  but it's not six inches."

Sarah always tried to show how much
she knew.

"Did everyone find a worm?"
  Mr. Bunsen asked.

"I didn't," said Adam.

"Neither did I," said Matt.

"You said you didn't like worms," said Sarah.
"Maybe that's why you didn't find one."

"Guess so," said Matt.

Sally called from the other side of the lot.
"Come here, everybody! Look what I found!"
Everyone ran to see what Sally had found.
It was a salamander.

"It's so cute!" said Jennifer.

"It is cute," said Mr. Bunsen. "But after
everyone has seen it, please put it back.
It will be hard to keep a salamander alive
in the classroom."

Chapter Four

Wiggle Wiggle

Back in the classroom, Mr. Bunsen gave everyone time to check their experiments. Jamie went to look at the handful of worms he had dumped in the dry dirt.

"Look at my worms," Jamie said. "They are all still there, except two."

Emily, who had put her worms in the wet dirt, said, "One of my worms crawled to the dry side. The rest are still where I put them."

Adam, who had put his worms in the middle, found his worms had all moved to the wet soil.

Jamie did some math in his head.
He said, "There are more worms in wet dirt than in dry dirt. So worms like wet better than dry. What I said before was right."

"Wait a minute," Mr. Bunsen said. "What about all those worms still in the dry soil?"

"They'll move," Jamie answered. "They're just slow."

"What if they don't?"

"I'm still right," said Jamie.

"You're stubborn," said Emily. "Just like my brother."

"How could you make Jamie change his mind?" Mr. Bunsen asked.

"By experimenting again," said Adam.

"Scientists repeat their experiments many times until they're sure," said Mr. Bunsen.

"Do we *have* to do this again?" asked Jamie.

"I think it would be a good idea," said Mr. Bunsen. "Why don't you put your box on the table by the window? Then you can check it later."

"Attention," called Mr. Bunsen.
"I've been talking to Adam, Emily, and Jamie.
  They're still not positive worms like wet dirt
  better than dry dirt, so they're going to repeat
  their experiments."

"How many times is enough?" asked Justin.
"Ten?"

"That sounds like a good number,"
  said Mr. Bunsen.

"Should we clean up?" Sarah asked.

"Yes, clean off the tables and put away
  the equipment."

"What about the worms?"

"Put them all back in the cooler,"
  said Mr. Bunsen, "and I'll give them a snack."

"What do worms eat?" asked Richard.

"Water and cornmeal," answered Mr. Bunsen.
"Doesn't that sound good?"

"NO!" yelled the class.

  Mr. Bunsen joked, "Well, then I guess
  we'll just have to have juice and cookies!"

"Hooray!"

"As soon as the room is clean!"
  Mr. Bunsen added.

Everyone wanted to eat, so cleanup went quickly. The snack helpers gave out the food. The classroom was pretty quiet. Everyone was busy eating. Suddenly there was a screech. "EEK!"

"What's wrong?" Mr. Bunsen asked.

"THERE'S A WORM UNDER MY PLATE!" Jennifer shouted.

"So, pick it up!" Adam yelled.

"Give it to me," said Mr. Bunsen.

Jennifer did not want to pick up the worm.
She was upset. She was sure someone had
put it there on purpose.

"What's wrong, Jennifer?" Mr. Bunsen asked.

Jennifer cried, "Richard left the worm there
to tease me."

"Did you?" Mr. Bunsen asked Richard.
Richard nodded.

Mr. Bunsen had a private talk with Richard.
Then Richard picked up the worm
and put it back in the cooler.
Wiggle. Wiggle.

Mr. Bunsen turned to the blackboard again. "We've asked ourselves a lot of questions about worms today. Can anyone give me some answers about worms?"

"Worms can sense what's around them," said Kelly.

"Worms like to hide under things," said Jennifer.

"Worms like water," said Jamie.

Adam said, "We still don't know that for sure."

"But you always see them in puddles," said Matt.

"And they live close to the top of the ground, where rain can get to them," added Emily.

"And Mr. Bunsen said they like water as a snack!" said Richard.

"Maybe Jamie was right," said Mr. Bunsen. "Worms seem to prefer wet over dry."

"*But*," Mr. Bunsen continued, "before we can say for sure, we'll have to do more experiments."

Jennifer raised her hand. "I learned something else about worms today," she said.

"And what's that?" Mr. Bunsen asked.

"They're not really *that* icky, but I still don't like them under my plate!"

Everybody laughed.

The bell rang.
It was time to go home.
"What are we going to do tomorrow?"
Sarah asked.

"I have something planned," Mr. Bunsen said,
"but I'm keeping my plans a secret."

"Please tell," begged Kelly.

"You can wait until tomorrow,"
said Mr. Bunsen.
"Class dismissed!"

Homework

- Go on a worm hunt near your house.

- Learn something new about a worm.

- Express your feelings about worms in 50 words or less.

Have fun!

Mr. Bunsen